Moving Pony

Do you love ponies? Be a Pony Pal!

Look for these Pony Pal books:

#1 I Want a Pony

#2 A Pony for Keeps

#3 A Pony in Trouble

#4 Give Me Back My Pony

#5 Pony to the Rescue

#6 Too Many Ponies

#7 Runaway Pony

#8 Good-bye Pony

#9 The Wild Pony

Super Special #1 The Baby Pony

#10 Don't Hurt My Pony

#11 Circus Pony

#12 Keep Out, Pony!

#13 The Girl Who Hated Ponies

#14 Pony-Sitters

Super Special #2 The Story of Our Ponies

#15 The Blind Pony

#16 The Missing Pony Pal

#17 Detective Pony

#18 The Saddest Pony

coming soon

#20 Stolen Ponies

Pony Pals

Moving Pony

Jeanne Betancourt

illustrated by Vivien Kubbos

SCHOLASTIC INC.
New York Toronto London Auckland Sydney
Mexico City New Delhi Hong Kong

ISBN 0-590-63397-X

12 11 10 9 8 7 6 5 4 3 2 9/9 0 1 2 3 4/0

Printed in the U.S.A. 40

First Scholastic printing, February 1999
Cover and text illustrations by Vivien Kubbos
Typeset in Bookman

Contents

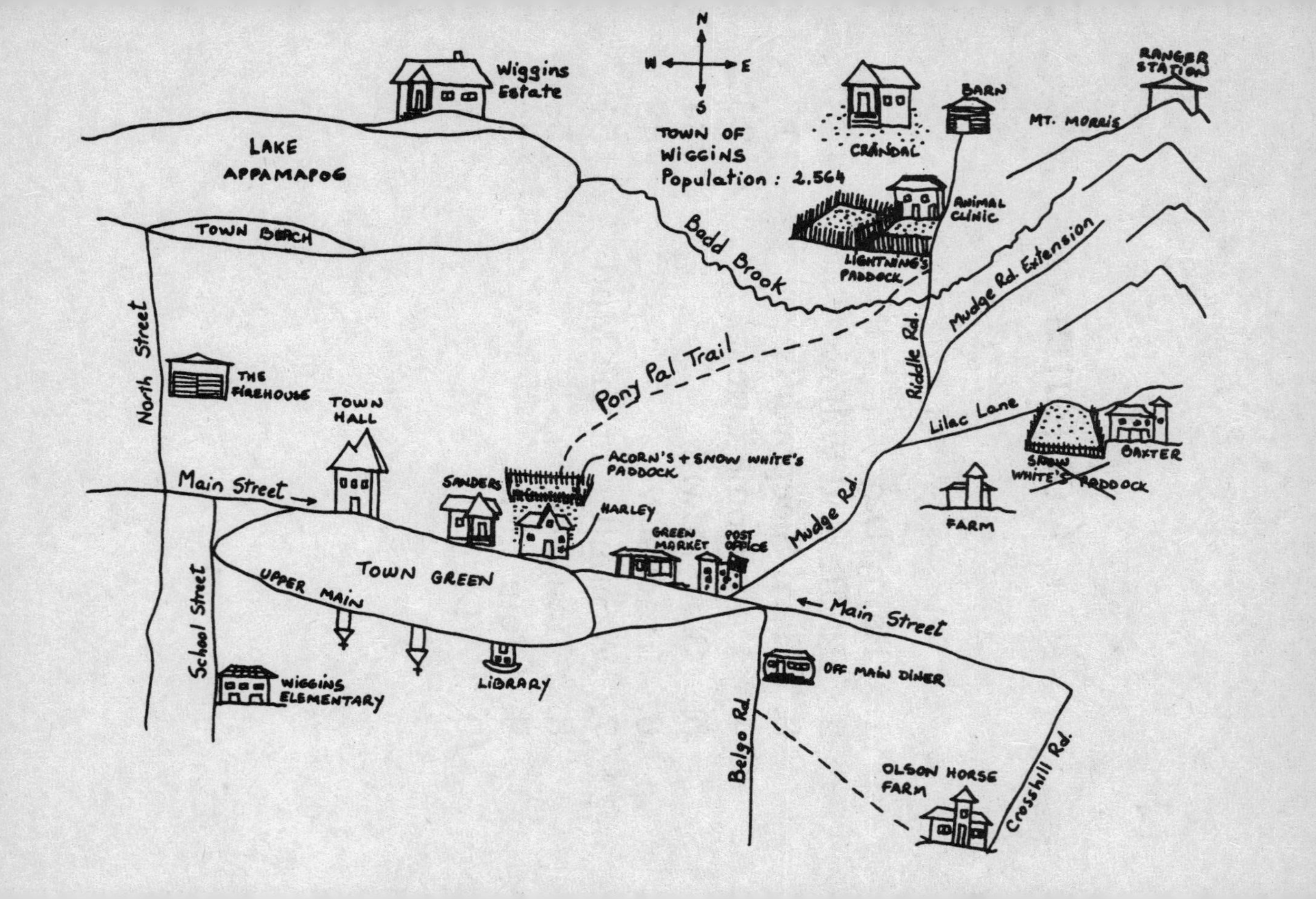

N
W
E
S
TOWN OF
WIGGINS
Population : 2,564
Wiggins Estate
LAKE APPAMAPOG
TOWN BEACH
CRANDAL
BARN
RANGER STATION
MT. MORRIS
ANIMAL CLINIC
LIGHTNING'S PADDOCK
Badd Brook
Mudge Rd. Extension
Riddle Rd.
Pony Pal Trail
Lilac Lane
BAXTER
SNOW WHITE'S PADDOCK
FARM
North Street
THE FIREHOUSE
TOWN HALL
Main Street
SANDERS
ACORN'S + SNOW WHITE'S PADDOCK
HARLEY
GREEN MARKET
POST OFFICE
Mudge Rd.
TOWN GREEN
UPPER MAIN
School Street
WIGGINS ELEMENTARY
LIBRARY
Main Street
OFF MAIN DINER
Belgo Rd.
OLSON HORSE FARM
Crosshill Rd.

Rainy Day

Lulu Sanders ran down Main Street through the heavy rain. Lulu's pony, Snow White, and her stable mate, Acorn, were almost out of oats. Lulu was going to buy them their favorite food.

She ran behind the Green Market towards Folger's Feed Store. Lulu slowed down when she saw a pony and a horse tied to the store's porch rail. The gray pony and brown horse were loaded down with camping equipment.

Lulu went inside the store. She wondered

who was camping in the rain. She soon spotted a woman and girl in yellow rain gear. They were looking at hoof picks.

"I don't know how I could have lost that pick," the woman said. "I'm sorry we had to ride so far without one."

"I told you it would be an awful trip," said the girl. "I want to go home."

"We can't, Sandy," the woman replied. "You know that. Try to look at the bright side."

"Mom, for me there is no bright side."

Sandy turned and came face to face with Lulu. Lulu smiled at her. Sandy didn't smile back. But when the woman passed Lulu, she said hello and they exchanged smiles.

Lulu went to the front of the store and ordered oats. She looked at her watch. She was late for her lunch date with her Pony Pals, Anna and Pam. When she left the store the horse and pony were still out front.

Lulu looked up at the dark, rainy sky. It

would rain for a long time. She knew that horses and ponies didn't mind the rain. But she felt sorry for Sandy and her mother. It wasn't fun to camp in the rain. Especially when one of the campers was in a bad mood.

Lulu tightened the hood on her slicker and headed towards the diner.

Anna's mother owned Off Main Diner. A lot of Pony Pal Meetings were held there.

Anna and Pam were already in the Pony Pals' favorite booth. They waved. "We've put in our orders," Anna called out. "Tell the cook what you want."

Lulu ordered a grilled cheese-and-tomato sandwich and went over to the booth. She sat down and told Pam and Anna about the mother and daughter campers on horseback.

Anna pointed out the window. "Is that them?" she asked.

The Pony Pals watched Sandy and her mother tie their pony and horse to the hitching post and walk towards the diner.

"Sandy looks like she's about our age," Anna said.

"It must be hard to camp in the rain," added Pam.

"I wonder how long they've been camping," said Lulu.

Sandy and her mother came into the restaurant and looked around. The only empty table was right next to the Pony Pals' booth. Sandy's mother recognized Lulu and smiled at her. Lulu smiled back and said hello.

The newcomers came over to the empty table and took off their rain gear. "The weather will be better tomorrow," Sandy's mother told her daughter.

"This whole thing was a terrible idea," said Sandy. "Why did we have to leave Powell? It's not fair."

The Pony Pals exchanged a glance. Lulu wondered where Powell was and why Sandy and her mother had to leave. How long had they been camping? Lulu knew that Anna and Pam were thinking about the mysterious travelers, too. But the Pony Pals couldn't talk about Sandy and her mother without being overheard by them.

Sandy and her mother placed their orders, and then went to the rest room. The Pony Pals leaned forward.

"Where's Powell?" asked Lulu.

"It's a small town about twenty-five miles south of here," answered Pam.

"That means they've been camping out for a few days already," Lulu said.

"That girl is very grumpy," observed Anna.

"You'd be grumpy, too," said Lulu, "if you were camping in the rain."

"I wonder where they're going," said Pam.

"Maybe they're not going anywhere," suggested Anna. "Maybe they're just running away."

"Maybe they're running from the law," said Pam. "Maybe they're criminals."

"Sh-hh," whispered Lulu. "Here they come. Change the subject."

"Well, I sure am hungry," announced Anna.

"Me, too," said Pam.

Lulu glanced at Sandy and her mother. Sandy still looked unhappy. Her mother looked worried and a little sad.

Who were they? wondered Lulu. And why did they leave Powell on horseback?

Raffle and Willow

Lulu felt sorry for Sandy's mother. She leant in her direction. "Don't worry about your horse and pony," she said. "We can see them from our booth. We'll keep an eye on them for you."

"Thank you," replied the woman. "That's very kind of you."

"The pony looks like a Connemara," said Pam.

"It is," said the woman. "His name is Raffle. My horse is named Willow. I'm Maria Nation. This is my daughter, Sandy."

"I'm Pam Crandal. My Connemara is named Lightning."

"Hi. I'm Anna Harley," said Anna with a little wave. "I have a Shetland pony named Acorn."

"And I'm Lulu Sanders. Snow White is my pony. She's a Welsh pony."

Lulu noticed that Sandy didn't smile once. Or say anything. Maybe she's shy, thought Lulu.

"Can we give Willow and Raffle apples?" asked Anna. "This is my mother's diner. We give our ponies apples from here all the time."

"They would love that," said Maria. "And thank you for talking to us. We've been out on the trail for a few days."

"Why don't you push your table next to our booth," suggested Anna. "Then we can all have lunch together."

"What a good idea," said Maria. "Let's do it."

Pam helped Maria push the table over to the booth.

"I'll get the apples," said Anna.

Lulu put on her raincoat and went out in the rain to give Raffle and Willow their treat. Lulu remembered the first time she brought apples to Lightning, Acorn and Snow White at that very same hitching post. She didn't know then how much she would love living in Wiggins.

When Lulu Sanders was three years old, her mother died. Since then Lulu had traveled all over the world with her father. Mr. Sanders studied wild animals and wrote about them. Lulu loved traveling with her father. But when she turned ten, her father wanted her to live in one place. That's when Lulu moved to Wiggins to live with her grandmother Sanders.

Lulu thought living in Wiggins would be boring. But that was before she met her Pony Pals.

Anna and Pam had lived in Wiggins all their lives. They'd been best friends since kindergarten.

Anna Harley lived next-door to Lulu's

grandmother. Anna was the most fun-loving girl Lulu had ever met. She was also the best artist. Lulu especially loved Anna's drawings of ponies. But Anna didn't like school. She was dyslexic, so reading and writing were hard subjects for her.

Pam, on the other hand, loved school. It was easy for her to earn good grades. Of all the Pony Pals, Pam knew the most about horses and ponies. Pam's father was a veterinarian and her mother had a riding school. Pam had been around ponies and horses all her life.

Lulu gave the apples to Raffle and Willow and ran back inside. She joined her Pony Pals and the Nations.

At first everyone talked about the good food at the diner. But Lulu wanted to find out more about the Nations and their mysterious camping trip.

"I'm sorry it's raining during your camping trip," Lulu told Maria.

"Hopefully the weather will improve tomorrow," said Maria.

"How long have you been on the trail?" asked Pam.

"Too long," mumbled Sandy.

"Three days," answered Maria. "The first two days we had perfect weather. We're trail riding and camping all the way to Reston. We should be there in two days."

"How will you get back to Powell?" asked Anna.

"We're not going back," said Sandy. Lulu thought she sounded angry.

"We're moving to Reston on horseback," explained Maria. "My husband and Sandy's brothers are driving our car. Since we don't have a horse trailer, Sandy and I decided to ride to Reston.

"YOU decided," said Sandy. This time Lulu was certain that she was angry.

"Now, Sandy," Maria said. "It hasn't all been bad. The camping site near Ritter River was delightful. That was just yesterday. Remember?"

Sandy didn't say anything.

"There was a calm pool at a bend in the

river," Maria told the Pony Pals. "It was clean and not too deep, so we went for a swim."

"Where's your next stop?" Pam asked Maria.

"We won't go much farther today because of the rain," said Maria. "I read about a shelter near Mt. Morris. I thought we might camp there. If Willow's okay."

"What's wrong with Willow?" asked Anna.

"He's been favoring his back right leg," Maria answered. "The salesperson at the Feed Store told me about a vet on Riddle Road." She reached in her pocket. "They gave me his card. I should call him right now."

"That's Pam's father!" exclaimed Anna. "He's the vet on Riddle Road."

"And he has office hours this afternoon," Pam said. "I'll call and tell him you're coming in."

While Pam phoned her father, Anna and Lulu cleared the table and made up a plate of brownies.

Pam had a huge smile on her face when she came back to the booth. "My dad says he can look at Willow at two o'clock. And my mother said you should stay overnight at our place."

"Our ponies are already at Pam's," said Anna. "We're sleeping there, too. We're having a barn sleepover tonight."

"Sandy, you can sleep with us in the barn," suggested Pam. "And your mother can stay in my room in the house."

"That's very kind," said Maria. "But we don't want to be any trouble."

"You won't be," said Pam. "My mom recognized your name. Did you win the Mt. Powell Endurance Ride last year?"

"I did," said Maria.

"My mother is a riding teacher," said Pam. "She said she'd love to talk to you about endurance riding."

"In that case we accept your invitation," said Maria with a smile.

Sandy suddenly stood up and pushed back her chair. "Can I call Liana now?" she asked her mother. "You said I could." Lulu noticed that Sandy was twisting a handmade, multi-colored string bracelet around her wrist.

"Honey, don't you think it will just make you sadder?" said Maria.

"You said I could call her after lunch," insisted Sandy. "You promised."

The Pony Pals exchanged a glance.

Who was Liana and why would talking to her make Sandy sad?

Barn Sleepover

The Pony Pals and Maria and Sandy Nation walked to the Crandals' after lunch. Sandy and Maria led Willow and Raffle. Pam's mother was waiting for them when they got to the barn. Lulu shook the rain off her slicker and went inside. She was glad to be in the dry barn.

Pam introduced Maria and Sandy to her mother. Mrs. Crandal and Maria recognized one another from the Eastern Division riding competitions. They were happy to be meeting again.

"Let's bring Willow to a stall in the new barn," Mrs. Crandal told Maria. "My husband will see him there."

"We'll help Sandy with Raffle," said Pam.

Sandy took off Raffle's saddle, while Pam took off the bridle.

"I'll clean the bridle," Lulu told Pam.

"And we'll help groom Raffle," said Pam.

Lulu took the bridle into the tack room. She thought, if we help Sandy she'll know we want to be friends. Then maybe she'll stop acting so shy and grumpy.

Lulu decided to give the bridle an extra-special cleaning. First, she took the bridle apart. Then she cleaned it and rubbed it with oil. She could hear the other girls talking while they worked on Sandy's pony.

"You're not supposed to use the curry comb when a pony is wet," Sandy told Anna.

"We always curry first," said Anna. "Even if the pony is wet."

"Well, that's the wrong way," said Sandy. "Everybody knows that."

Lulu knew that Anna had a quick temper. She didn't want Anna to argue with Sandy, so she yelled, "Anna, can you help me in here?"

"Sure," Anna yelled back.

Anna came into the tack room. She leant over and whispered to Lulu, "That Sandy is so bossy."

"I heard," said Lulu.

Sandy came into the tack room, too. She looked at the bridle pieces. "What did you do to my bridle?" she asked angrily.

"I'm cleaning it," explained Lulu.

"But you took it apart," said Sandy. "You're not supposed to take a bridle apart when you clean it."

"Everybody knows that," said Anna, imitating Sandy.

Sandy glared at Anna. "Well, everybody *should* know it," Sandy said.

"Hi there," a man's voice called out. It was Dr. Crandal.

"Come on," Lulu said to Anna and Sandy. "Let's find out about Willow."

Dr. Crandal told the girls that Willow was lame. "He needs to rest for a day or so," he said. Then he ran his hand along Raffle's neck. "How's this pony doing?" he asked.

The Pony Pals and Sandy watched as Dr. Crandal felt Raffle's limbs and listened to his heart and lungs. "Looks like he's in great shape," Dr. Crandal concluded. "How has he seemed to you?" he asked Sandy.

"He's been a little sad," Sandy answered.

"Why is that?" asked Dr. Crandal.

Sandy brushed out Raffle's brown mane with her fingers. "He didn't want to leave his friends in Powell," said Sandy. "That's why he's sad."

Dr. Crandal put the stethoscope in his jacket pocket. "He'll soon make new friends in Reston," he told her.

"No, he won't," Lulu heard Sandy mumble to herself.

After Dr. Crandal left, Pam and Sandy finished grooming Raffle.

Lulu put Raffle's bridle back together and Anna went out to the big paddock to check

on Snow White, Lightning and Acorn.

"We can put Raffle out in the small paddock for the night," Pam told Sandy. "It's right next to the big paddock. That way your pony can make friends with our ponies."

"I want him to stay inside in a stall tonight," said Sandy.

"It's stopped raining," Lulu pointed out.

"He might like to be outside with the other ponies," added Pam.

"I said I want him to stay in a stall tonight," repeated Sandy.

Lulu thought, *Sandy doesn't want Raffle to make new friends.*

That night the Crandals served up a huge spaghetti dinner. Lulu noticed that everyone was having a great time together—everyone but Sandy.

The four girls did the dishes. When they finished, Anna suggested that they all go to the barn office and play cards.

"I don't like to play cards," said Sandy.

"I'll stay here and watch television until it's time to go to bed."

Anna turned to Lulu and Pam. "Do you guys want to play?" she asked.

Pam and Lulu exchanged a glance. They wanted to play cards and get away from Sandy's bad mood.

"Sure," said Lulu.

"All right," agreed Pam.

"We usually go to bed around ten o'clock," Lulu told Sandy. "Is that okay with you?"

"I don't go to bed until ten-thirty," said Sandy. "You sleep better if you go to bed late."

Lulu couldn't believe it. Sandy thought that everything she did was the best way—even the hour she went to bed.

Anna grabbed Lulu by the hand and the three Pony Pals left the house.

"She is driving me crazy," said Anna as soon as they were outside.

"They'll leave in the morning," said Pam.

"Good riddance," said Anna. "I can't wait

until she's gone."

"And tomorrow we'll go on a long trail ride," added Lulu.

The girls went to the barn office and unrolled their sleeping bags. Pam laid out her mother's sleeping bag for Sandy. They carefully arranged the four bags in a circle with the feet end pointing towards the center of the room. Then they sat cross-legged in the circle at the foot of their bags. Pam dealt the cards.

"Sandy reminds me of Rema Baxter," said Anna. "They both act as if they know more than anybody else."

"Let's forget about Sandy and have some fun," said Lulu.

For two hours the Pony Pals played cards. They joked and laughed and forgot about Sandy. When they were tired, they crawled into their sleeping bags.

Pam and Anna were sound asleep when Sandy came in, but Lulu was still awake. She kept her eyes closed and listened. First she heard Sandy turn off the light and get into her sleeping bag. Then she heard the short breaths of Sandy crying.

Lulu felt sorry for Sandy. She knew she was upset about moving. Lulu wondered if she should say something to Sandy. But she couldn't think of what to say to the unfriendly girl.

Finally the crying sounds changed into the long deep breaths of sleeping. And then Lulu fell asleep, too.

Unwelcome Guest

The next morning the Pony Pals woke up before Sandy. They dressed quietly and went outside to feed their ponies. The sky was blue and clear, and the air was warm. It was a perfect day for a trail ride.

"Sandy cried herself to sleep last night," Lulu told Pam and Anna.

"She doesn't want to move to Reston," said Anna.

Lulu laid her cheek on Snow White's smooth neck. "Let's try to be nice to her," she suggested. "Moving to a new place can be scary."

"There she is," whispered Pam.

Lulu saw Sandy standing in the doorway to the barn. The three girls went over to say good morning to their guest.

"We're going to the house for breakfast," Pam told Sandy.

"I have to feed Raffle," Sandy told her.

"Don't worry, we'll wait for you," said Lulu.

"Don't bother," Sandy said. She turned and went back into the barn.

"I don't think she knows how to make new friends," said Pam.

"That's for sure!" exclaimed Anna.

At breakfast, Lulu sat next to Sandy. "It's a nice day for riding," Lulu commented. "A lot better than yesterday."

"Yeah," said Sandy.

"How's Raffle today?" asked Lulu.

"Okay," Sandy answered.

Lulu tried some more questions, but Sandy always answered with one word. Lulu finally gave up trying to talk to her.

Dr. Crandal and Maria Nation came into the kitchen from outside. Dr. Crandal poured them both a cup of coffee and sat down next to Mrs. Crandal. Maria sat down next to Sandy. Lulu handed Maria a plate of blueberry muffins.

"How's Willow?" Mrs. Crandal asked.

"He's better than he was yesterday," said Maria.

"But I think he should rest for another day," added Dr. Crandal.

"It looks like you're stuck here with us, Maria," said Mrs. Crandal.

"I don't mind," said Maria. "I'll watch you teach and get some more ideas on how to run a riding school. Besides, I like making new friends."

"Me, too," said Mrs. Crandal.

The two women smiled at one another.

Why can't Sandy be more like her mother? thought Lulu.

Mrs. Crandal turned to Sandy. "Now you can go on the trail ride with the other girls," she told her.

Lulu's heart sank. She didn't want Sandy on their trail ride. She would ruin all their fun.

"I don't want to go on a trail ride," said Sandy. "Raffle and I want to rest, too."

Good, thought Lulu.

"Well, maybe you three should stick around here then," Mrs. Crandal told the Pony Pals.

"No," said Sandy. "They can go. I want them to go. I want to be alone."

Lulu saw the sad look on Maria's face again.

"Where are you girls riding today?" asked Dr. Crandal.

"Ritter Trail," said Pam.

"We thought we'd find the swimming place on the river that Maria told us about," said Lulu.

"Is it too far for one day?" Pam asked Maria.

"No," said Maria, "as long as you're experienced riders."

"They are all excellent riders," said Mrs. Crandal proudly.

"I didn't know you were going *there*," Sandy said excitedly. "That's a great trail. I'll go with you after all, if it's okay."

Lulu didn't want Sandy to be on their trail ride, but she remembered how Sandy had cried herself to sleep. Lulu felt sorry for her. "Of course it's okay," she told Sandy. "You can show us the way."

"We'll have fun," added Pam.

Lulu and Anna looked at each other. They didn't think that Sandy Nation knew how to have fun.

The four girls packed lunches of peanut butter and jelly sandwiches, cookies and apples. Lulu was surprised that Sandy wanted three sandwiches. She also took more cookies than anyone else. Lulu decided that Sandy Nation had a big appetite.

The four girls went back to the barn and put their swimsuits on under their clothes.

"We should introduce Raffle to our ponies before they go on a trail ride together," said Pam.

Everyone agreed.

The Pony Pals went
clipped lead lines on
while Sandy got one for R

"Let's introduce Acorn first,"
Pam. "He's the friendliest pony in the world."

They walked the three ponies towards the entrance of the small paddock. Sandy and Raffle were waiting for them. When Acorn saw Raffle he nickered as if to say, "Oh, good, a new friend."

Anna brought him closer. Acorn reached out with his nose to sniff Raffle's face. Raffle pinned his ears back, spun around and tried to kick Acorn.

Sandy tightened her hold on Raffle and Anna quickly pulled Acorn away.

Lightning whinnied fearfully and backed away from the unfriendly pony.

Snow White tugged on the lead to go closer to Raffle, but Lulu pulled her back.

Maybe Sandy will change her mind about going on the trail ride, thought Lulu. She hoped so.

"Why did Acorn attack Raffle?" asked Sandy.

"He did not attack Raffle," Anna said angrily. "It was the other way around."

"Raffle tried to kick Acorn," said Pam calmly.

"Maybe Raffle is upset because he saw three ponies," suggested Lulu. "He felt outnumbered three-to-one."

"He always got on well with all of my friends' ponies in Powell," said Sandy. "Especially Liana's pony, Peaches."

"Maybe we shouldn't go on a long trail ride today," said Lulu. "We can do a short ride around here instead."

"But I want to go back to Ritter Trail," Sandy said. "I'll keep Raffle away from your ponies." She patted Raffle's cheek. "You'll be a good boy, won't you, Raffle?"

Raffle doesn't like our ponies, thought Lulu. And Sandy doesn't like us. So why does she want to go on this trail ride?

Slow Down!

The four girls went into the barn for their saddles. Lulu noticed Sandy's bracelet again. "Your bracelet is pretty," she told her. "I love all the colors. Did someone make it for you?"

"Liana made it," she said. "Liana's my best friend in my whole life. Everyone thinks we're sisters. Her parents wanted me to live with them. They didn't want me to move to Reston."

"I'm sorry you have to move," said Lulu.

Lulu saw tears collect in Sandy's eyes.

Sandy turned and walked towards Raffle. *Sandy doesn't want me to see her cry,* thought Lulu.

Lulu put on Snow White's saddle and bridle. As she worked she thought about how unhappy she'd be if she had to leave Anna and Pam.

Each girl put their lunch and drinking water, a towel and sweatshirt in their saddle bags. Pam put the first-aid kit in her bag. Lulu had the hoof pick and Anna had the flashlight. Lulu patted her pocket to be sure she had her whistle.

Finally, the four riders pulled down their stirrups and mounted their ponies.

"I'll go first," Sandy told the Pony Pals, "so your ponies don't upset Raffle."

Anna glared at Sandy, but she didn't say anything.

Sandy and Raffle led the way. Pam followed behind Sandy. Lulu came next and Anna last. They rode down Riddle Road onto Mudge Road and along Main Street. The parade of ponies turned left onto

School Street. Soon they reached the entrance to Ritter Trail and headed into the woods.

Lulu enjoyed the ride along the old woodland trail. She loved to swim and was looking forward to being in the river.

The girls trotted and galloped their ponies on the straight, dry stretches of trail. But when the trail got muddy, they slowed down.

Suddenly Pam yelled to Sandy, "Hey, wait up!"

Lulu looked ahead. She could see Pam, but she couldn't see Sandy.

"Let's catch up with her," Lulu shouted to Pam.

Pam galloped Lightning along a straight, firm stretch of trail. Lulu and Anna followed on their ponies. "Sandy, slow down," Pam yelled.

Sandy was waiting for them at the next turn in the trail. "What's the problem?" she asked.

"We couldn't see you," explained Pam.

“So what?” snapped Sandy.

“You’re going too fast,” said Pam. “You should slow down when the trail is muddy. It’s dangerous to gallop in mud.”

“Besides, we’re supposed to stick together,” added Lulu.

“Don’t you know the way to the pool?” Sandy asked.

“Not really,” said Anna.

“We’ve never been there before,” added Lulu.

Raffle took a couple of steps towards Acorn. Acorn’s ears immediately went back and he snorted a warning to Raffle. Lightning pawed the ground nervously.

Sandy pulled Raffle back. “We’ll lead you there then,” she said. She turned Raffle back on the trail and started off again.

The Pony Pals followed Sandy on the trail for almost an hour. Lulu’s hair felt damp under her helmet. Her whole body was sticky with sweat. She couldn’t wait to jump into the river.

“We’re almost there,” Sandy yelled. She

made a sharp right onto a smaller trail. In a few minutes the four ponies and their riders stood beside the river. Lulu could see their reflections in a wide, calm pool of water. It was a perfect place for a swim.

She slid off Snow White. “Let’s swim before lunch,” she suggested.

They all agreed. But first they let their ponies drink from the river.

Sandy kept Raffle away from the other ponies. But Snow White watched every move Raffle made. Lulu wondered if her pony was afraid of Raffle or just curious.

Pam pointed to a stand of three trees. “We’ll use those trees for hitching our ponies,” she told Sandy. “You can use any of the other trees for Raffle.”

“I’m not hitching him to a tree,” Sandy told them, “because I’m not staying.”

“You’re not?” said Lulu and Anna together.

“Why not?” asked Pam.

“I just came to show you the way,” she said. She patted Raffle’s side. “And to give

Raffle a little exercise."

"Aren't you hot?" asked Lulu.

"I thought you liked swimming here," added Pam.

"I don't like swimming that much," said Sandy.

"What about lunch?" asked Lulu.

"I'm not hungry," Sandy replied.

"But we want to stay," Anna told Sandy. "It's three against one."

Sandy smiled at Anna. It was the first time Lulu had ever seen Sandy smile. "You stay and swim and have a wonderful time," she said in a pleasant voice. "I'll go back alone. I don't mind." Sandy smiled at Lulu and Pam, too. "Thank you for inviting me," she said. "I had fun."

Sandy put her foot in the stirrup and swung onto the saddle. She gave Pam an extra-special smile. "Can we sleep in the barn again tonight?" she asked.

"Sure," said Pam.

"Great," said Sandy. "See you later."

She waved goodbye and rode away.

Acorn nickered as if to say, "Good riddance."

"Did you see that?" asked Anna. "Sandy actually smiled at us."

"I guess she likes us after all," said Pam.

"If she likes us, why did she leave?" asked Lulu.

"I don't care why she left," said Anna. "I'm just glad she's gone. Now we can have some fun."

"She shouldn't be riding so far alone," Pam said. "It's not safe."

"If she runs into trouble," said Anna, "we'll find her. There's only one way back." She pulled off her T-shirt and jeans. "Last one in is a rotten egg," she shouted.

Soon the three girls were splashing and swimming in the cool pool.

Lulu dived under the water and swam along the bottom of the river. She stood on her hands. Then she floated on her back and watched a white, puffy cloud change shape. As Lulu watched the cloud she wondered, why did Sandy start acting friendly towards us? Why did she want to go back to the Crandals'?

Tracks

After the swim, the Pony Pals took their lunches out of their saddle bags. They sat on rocks at the edge of the river to eat.

"I'm glad Sandy didn't stay," Anna said.

"But she was being nice to us at last," said Pam.

"That wasn't real," said Anna. "She was just *acting* nice."

Lulu picked up a flat stone and skipped it across the water. "I agree with Anna," she said. "But there's something I don't understand. Why was Sandy pretending to like us?"

"Let's go back," said Pam. "We'll see if she's still nice to us. Maybe she likes us, after all."

Anna and Lulu agreed. They were curious to see how Sandy would act, too.

The three girls dressed, packed their saddle bags and prepared their ponies. Soon they were riding back towards Wiggins. This time Anna led the way, Lulu followed and Pam rode last.

When they came to a muddy stretch of trail, Anna slowed Acorn to a walk. After a few steps she brought him to a stop. She turned to Lulu and pointed at the mud. "Look at these tracks," she said. "What are they?"

Lulu and Pam pulled their ponies up beside Acorn. Lulu leaned over and studied the tracks.

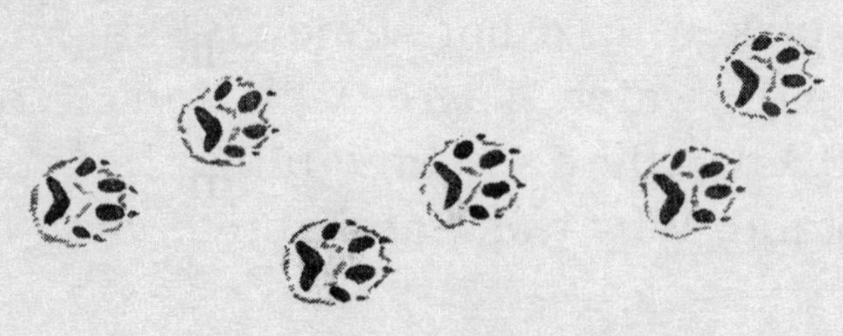

"They're red fox prints," Lulu told Anna. "See the hairy imprint around the edges. Red fox have fur on the bottom of their paws. And look at the boomerang shape at the back. A red fox was here."

"Wow," said Anna.

"You are a good animal tracker, Lulu," said Pam.

"And a great detective," added Anna.

The Pony Pals rode on.

Lulu thought, I *am* a detective and there is a mystery to be solved here. The mystery of Sandy Nation.

Lulu kept her eyes on the muddy trail ahead of them. They were full of hoof prints. But something was wrong about those prints. Something was missing.

"Anna," she called ahead. "Stop Acorn for a second."

Anna halted Acorn. Lulu pulled Snow White up beside him.

Pam halted Lightning behind them. "What's wrong?"

"I don't know," said Lulu. "I want to study the tracks." She slid off Snow White and handed the reins to Anna.

"The fox was crossing the trail," said Anna. "He didn't go straight."

"I'm not looking for the fox tracks," explained Lulu. "I want to study the hoof prints."

"There are a lot of those," said Anna.

Anna was right. The mud was covered with hoof prints.

Lulu squatted and studied them.

"Those are the prints we made on our way to the river," said Anna.

Lulu stood up. "That's right," she said. "And all of them are going in the same direction. South."

"What's wrong with that?" asked Anna. "We were riding south."

"Yes," Lulu replied, "but to go home we're riding north."

"And if Sandy rode back ahead of us," added Pam, "we should see Raffle's hoof prints going north."

"Aren't any of them going towards Wiggins?" asked Anna.

"Not that I can see," answered Lulu. "I'm going to walk ahead and study more tracks. Just to be sure."

Lulu kept her eyes on the mud as she walked. She didn't see even one track going north. She ran back to her friends.

"Sandy didn't ride this way," she told them.

"I wonder where she went," said Pam.

"Is there another way to get back to Wiggins?" asked Anna.

Pam thought for a moment. "I don't think so," she answered. "I've never heard about one. And I rode here a lot with my mother when I was little."

"Maybe we should go back to the river," suggested Anna.

"And try to track her from there," said Pam.

"Good idea," said Lulu. She swung up onto Snow White.

"You lead the way back," Pam told Lulu.

"You might spot a clue."

"We should all look for clues," Lulu said. "Pam, you look to the right."

"I'll look to the left," said Anna.

"And I'll look in front of us," added Lulu. She pulled ahead of her friends and led at a walk. Whenever the trail was muddy she halted. "I'm looking to see if there are any tracks leading off the trail," she explained to Anna and Pam.

But there were no hoof prints leading off the trail.

Lulu suddenly remembered something that her father told her. "If you're tracking, pretend you are the animal or person you're tracking."

I'm Sandy Nation, thought Lulu. Sad, lonely thoughts filled Lulu's head. *I don't want to move to Reston. I want to be with my old friends. Especially Liana. She's my best friend in the whole world. My parents can't make me move. They can't. I want to go back to Powell and live with Liana.*

Lulu and Snow White reached the turn-off to Ritter River. She halted Snow White. Anna and Pam pulled up behind her.

Lulu turned in the saddle. "I'm going back to Powell," she told them.

"What?" asked Pam.

"You're going *where*?" asked Anna.

"I'm positive. Sandy is riding back to Powell. I'm sure she rode south instead of north. That's why we didn't see her tracks."

"What will she do when she gets there?" asked Anna. "Her parents and brothers are moving to Reston."

"She said she can live with Liana's family," said Lulu.

"But it's a two-day ride," said Pam.

"And she doesn't have any camping equipment," Anna added.

"But she has loads of food," Lulu reminded them. "Remember how much food she packed? She planned this."

"*That's* why she was being nice to us," said Anna. "So we wouldn't guess."

"Let's ride south for a little while," said Lulu. "I bet we'll see fresh hoof prints on the trail."

The Pony Pals rode south. Lulu kept her eyes on the packed dirt in front of them. Soon she saw hoof prints and a fresh pile of pony plop.

I was right, thought Lulu. Sandy *is* riding back to Powell. Now what are we going to do?

7

A Smudge in the Mud

The Pony Pals pulled their ponies up to the hoof prints and pony plop.

"The hoof prints are pony size," said Anna.

"And we haven't seen anyone else riding today," said Lulu. "This is evidence that Sandy is riding south."

"What are we going to do?" asked Anna.

"Let's go back to my place," suggested Pam. "We have to tell Sandy's mother that she's run away." She began to turn Lightning around.

"Wait, Pam," said Lulu. "Let's try to find Sandy."

"We'll never catch up with her, Lulu," said Anna. "She's had a big head start."

"Maybe she stopped to rest or to have lunch," said Lulu. "I think we should try."

"I still think we should go back and tell her mother," insisted Pam.

"It's dangerous for her to be riding alone," said Lulu. "We should follow her . . . just in case she needs us."

"But she doesn't like us," said Anna. "Remember?"

Lulu thought for a few seconds. "I have a feeling that we should follow her anyway."

"What will we do if we find her?" asked Pam.

"Try to convince her to go back with us," said Lulu.

"Good luck!" exclaimed Anna. "She is *very* stubborn."

"We have to try," begged Lulu.

"Okay," said Pam. "We'll follow her tracks. But if we don't find her in an hour, we should go back. Agreed?"

"Agreed," said Lulu and Anna together.

Lulu led the way. She galloped Snow White on a long, dry stretch of trail. When they came to a muddy patch she slowed down. Raffle's prints were big and deep in the dark brown mud.

"Sandy was galloping here," Lulu told Pam and Anna.

"She's going too fast for the conditions," Pam pointed out. "It's very dangerous."

When they came to the next muddy patch, Snow White stopped abruptly. "What's wrong, Snow White?" Lulu asked. The pony lowered her head and sniffed the mud. Lulu leaned over and studied the spot Snow White was smelling.

"Don't bring your ponies over here," she told Anna and Pam. "They'll mess up the tracks. But come see this."

Pam and Anna slid off their ponies and walked over to Lulu. Lulu pointed at a big smudge in the mud. "Something happened here," she said.

“Maybe a fox had a fight with another animal,” said Anna.

Lulu studied the area around the smudge. “There aren’t any fox tracks.” She pointed to hoof prints in the mud. “The only animal that was here was a pony.”

Pam understood immediately. “Raffle fell,” she said.

“Poor Raffle!” exclaimed Anna.

“It was Sandy’s fault,” said Pam. “She was going too fast.”

“I hope Raffle wasn’t hurt,” Anna said.

“Let’s see if we can find more tracks,” suggested Lulu.

The three girls led their ponies. The trail was dry again. But Lulu still looked for clues. Finally they came to a damp spot, and Lulu saw what she was looking for—a set of clean hoof prints. She pointed them out to Pam and Anna.

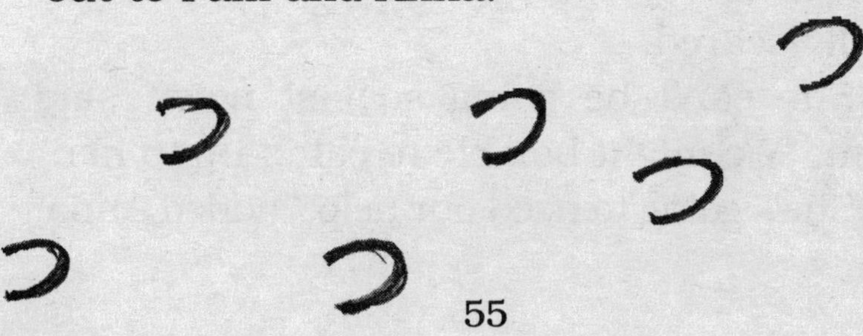

"These prints are evenly spaced," Lulu said.

"And none of them has a drag mark," added Anna.

"That means Raffle isn't limping," concluded Pam.

"Look!" exclaimed Lulu. She pointed to boot prints in the mud.

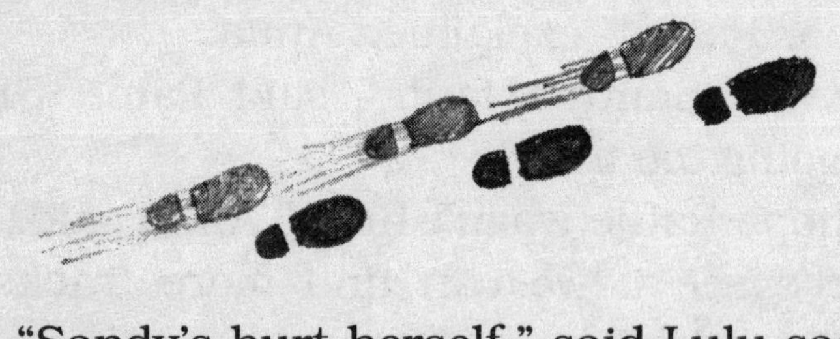

"Sandy's hurt herself," said Lulu sadly.

"I bet she's sprained her ankle," said Pam. She bent over the tracks. "It's her left foot. She can't get back onto Raffle."

"A sprained ankle hurts," said Anna. "Especially if you try to walk on it."

Poor Sandy, thought Lulu. She must be really scared.

"She can't be going so fast now," said Pam. "We might be able to catch up to her."

"She's going to need our help," added Anna.

"Come on," said Lulu as she jumped up onto Snow White.

The girls rode for another fifteen minutes. Lulu concentrated on looking for fresh tracks.

Suddenly the trail forked.

"Which way do you think she went?" asked Pam.

"I don't know," sighed Lulu.

"The trail is grassy and dry here," said Anna. "I don't see tracks."

If I were Sandy, thought Lulu, which way would I go? And what if I'm found? Would I let three girls I don't like help me?

First Aid

"Let's use our whistles," suggested Pam. "That way Sandy will know we're looking for her."

"What if she doesn't *want* us to find her?" said Anna. "Then she'll hide from us. I think we need to sneak up on her."

Pam looked at the fork in the trail. "But which way should we go?"

"I'll check the beginning of both trails," Lulu said. "I'll bend close to the ground and look for evidence. Raffle and Sandy would have trampled grass and broken small twigs as they walked."

Snow White pulled on the reins. She wanted to go on the trail to the left. "I'll check the left one first," Lulu told her friends. "And I'll take Snow White with me. She's a good detective, too."

Lulu slid off Snow White and led her along the trail. She squatted down every few yards and studied the trail. The surface of the ground was hard. Lulu couldn't find any evidence that a pony and a limping girl had walked there. Suddenly Snow White nickered.

Lulu stood up. "What is it?" she asked. "Did something startle you?"

Lulu looked around. She noticed a colorful spot on a tree branch. "That's just a bird," she told Snow White. Lulu took a few steps forward to see what kind of bird it was. But the "bird" didn't fly away.

It's not a bird, thought Lulu. But what is it?

Lulu moved closer. It looked like a circle of colorful string. Lulu ran over to the branch and removed it. "It's Sandy's bracelet!" she exclaimed.

Lulu ran back to her friends. "Look," she said excitedly. "Sandy took the trail to the left. This trail."

"Do you think Sandy dropped her bracelet?" asked Anna. "Is it broken?"

"No," said Lulu. "It was hanging on a tree branch. She must have put it there. I think she wants us to find her."

"Let's go," said Anna.

"*And* we'll use our whistles," added Pam.

The three girls rode their ponies along the hard-packed trail. After a short distance they stopped. They blew their whistles and yelled, "Sandy." Then they kept very quiet . . . they were listening for Sandy's answer.

Snow White whinnied.

"Sh-h," Lulu told her pony. "We're listening for an answer."

But there was no answer to their calls.

The Pony Pals rode a little farther, then stopped. They sent out their signal again.

Snow White whinnied again.

"Snow White, be quiet," Pam said.

"Wait a minute," Lulu said. "Maybe Snow White is sending her own signal to Raffle."

Snow White nickered as if to say, "Of course that's what I'm doing."

The three girls yelled, "Sandy," and blew their whistles. Again Snow White whinnied. Then they were all quiet. This time they heard a faint whinny in the distance.

"Raffle!" exclaimed Anna.

Lulu patted Snow White's neck. "Go ahead, Snow White," she said. "Call her again."

Snow White whinnied. A whinny answered. This time it sounded closer.

Snow White nickered happily. The whinny that answered her was happy, too.

"Look!" exclaimed Anna. "There's Raffle, behind us."

Lulu turned around to see Raffle racing towards them. She jumped off Snow White and grabbed Raffle's halter. Lightning backed away and Acorn snorted. But Snow

White went right up to Raffle and the two ponies sniffed each other's faces.

Lulu patted Raffle's side. "Good pony," she said. "Now bring us to Sandy."

"She must have gone off the trail," said Pam. "Otherwise we would have passed her."

"I wonder why?" said Anna. "If she wanted us to find her, she would have stayed on the trail."

"I hope nothing terrible has happened to her," said Lulu. "Come on, let's go."

Raffle led the way back along the trail. After a few minutes he turned into the woods, along a deer run. The girls led their ponies under tree branches and through brambles.

"I wonder why she came in here?" said Anna.

"Maybe Raffle doesn't know where Sandy is, either," suggested Pam. "Maybe he's a runaway pony."

"Sandy," Lulu shouted, "where are you?"

"I'm here," a faint voice answered. "By the brook."

Raffle nickered. He is leading us to Sandy, thought Lulu.

The narrow path ended in a clearing, where a small brook ran through it. They saw Sandy sitting at the edge of the brook with her feet in the water.

Raffle and the Pony Pals ran over to her. Sandy looked up at them. "Hi," she said. "I knew you'd find me." She pointed to her foot. Lulu could see that it was very swollen.

"I've sprained my ankle," said Sandy. "Or maybe I've broken it."

"It looks like it hurts," said Anna.

"The cold water helps," she said. "It should help the swelling go down."

"Don't worry, Sandy," said Lulu. "We're here now. We'll get you safely back to the Crandals'."

"We have a big horse trailer," said Pam. "If you can't ride, my mom can drive Willow and Raffle to your new home."

"But I'm not going to my new home," said Sandy. "I'm going back to Powell, to live with Liana and her parents. I wanted you to find me because I need your help," she said. "I need your help to get to Powell."

The Pony Pals exchanged a glance. Sandy wanted them to help her *run away*. Should they help her?

Four Ideas

Sandy lifted her injured foot out of the water. "Do you have an ace bandage in your first aid kit?" she asked Pam.

"Yes," said Pam. "I'll get it."

"I can wrap the ace bandage around your ankle," Lulu told Sandy. "I know how."

Sandy smiled at Lulu. "Thanks," she said.

Pam handed Lulu the bandage.

"Pam and I will tie up our ponies," said Anna.

The two girls led the ponies away.

"I hoped you'd find me," Sandy told Lulu. "But I was afraid you'd go on the wrong trail. Did you find my bracelet?"

Lulu reached into her pocket and took out the bracelet. She handed it to Sandy. "Snow White saw it first," said Lulu. "It was a good clue." Sandy slid the bracelet over her hand onto her wrist.

"But why didn't you just stay on the trail?" Lulu asked.

"I remembered this brook," Sandy answered. "I wanted to soak my ankle in it."

Lulu knelt in front of Sandy and gently lifted her foot. "How does it feel?" she asked.

"It hurts a lot when I put weight on it," answered Sandy.

"I hope you haven't broken it," said Lulu.

"Me, too," said Sandy.

Lulu began wrapping the bandage around Sandy's swollen ankle.

Pam and Anna came back from tying up the ponies and sat on some rocks near

Sandy and Lulu. Pam held out Sandy's lunch bag. "I brought your lunch," she said. "In case you're hungry."

"I've eaten one sandwich already," said Sandy. "I'm saving the rest for dinner."

"We'll be home for dinner," said Anna.

"I told you, I'm not going back with you," said Sandy. "I'm going to Powell."

"How?" asked Anna. "You can't ride with a sprained ankle."

"That's why I need your help," said Sandy.

"But we're not going to Powell," said Pam. "*We're* not running away."

"I know," said Sandy. "But there are still things you can do to help me." She pulled a scrap of paper out of her pocket. "Back in Powell, whenever my three riding friends and I have problems, we write down ideas on how to solve them. So I pretended they were here with me. Then I thought of four ideas to solve this problem."

"That's what *we* do!" exclaimed Anna.

"There are three of us, so we only have three ideas," said Pam.

"And I always draw my idea," added Anna.

"We always come up with good ideas when we do that," said Lulu.

"So do we," said Sandy. "But I didn't know there were other riding friends who did it." Sandy was smiling. Lulu knew that it wasn't a pretend smile this time.

"What are your ideas?" Lulu asked.

Sandy handed her list to Lulu. "Here," she said. "You read them."

Lulu read Sandy's ideas out loud.

How Pam, Anna and Lulu can help me

1. Tell my mother that I am going back to Powell and that she should let me.
2. Don't tell my mother that I hurt my ankle.
3. Lend me their extra sweaters.
4. Telephone Liana Roberts in Powell (tel. #758-098). Tell her where I am. Ask her to come help Raffle and me.

"Will you do those things for me?" asked Sandy. "*Please.*"

The Pony Pals exchanged a glance. None of them wanted to leave Sandy alone in the woods, especially with a sprained ankle.

"We want to help you," said Lulu, "but we don't want to leave you here."

"Liana will come and get me tomorrow," said Sandy. "We went on a camping trip around here once. I'll tell you how to explain where I am."

"But what will you do tonight?" asked Lulu. "You can't stay in the woods alone at night."

"Yes, I can," said Sandy. "I'm not afraid. Besides, I'm not alone. I have Raffle."

Lulu wondered if *she* would be brave enough to stay in the woods alone at night. She wouldn't be afraid if Snow White was with her. But she *would* be afraid if she was injured.

"It's cold at night," said Pam.

"I'll lie on Raffle's saddle blanket," said Sandy. She pointed to the plaid saddle blanket spread out in the sun. "I'm drying it now. I have a big plastic bag to put under it. If you lend me your extra sweaters I'll be warm enough."

"Those are all good ideas," said Pam. "You *are* very adventurous."

"And brave," said Anna. She shuddered. "I could never stay in the woods alone. I'd be too afraid."

"Why aren't you brave about moving to Reston?" asked Pam. "Moving is an adventure, too."

"All my friends are in Powell," said Sandy.

"You can make new friends," Anna said.

Pam put her hand on Sandy's shoulder. "Making new friends can be fun," she said.

"But I don't want to," said Sandy. She looked sad again. "You don't know how hard it is to leave your friends. You've never had to do it."

"I have," said Lulu. "I've moved lots of times. I know it's hard."

"When Lulu moved she came all the way

from England," Anna said.

"She never sees her old friends, but you can. Reston and Powell aren't that far apart."

"And you have your pony," added Pam. "Raffle is moving with you."

Lulu finished wrapping Sandy's ankle. "Why can't you keep your old friends *and* make new ones?" Lulu asked as she stood up.

"Then you'll have twice as many friends," said Anna.

"You can talk on the phone with your friends in Powell," suggested Pam. "And even meet them on weekends."

"It's not the same," argued Sandy. "I've lived in Powell all my life. I love living there."

"I'm sure you'll make new friends fast," said Anna, encouragingly.

"Especially if your mom has a riding school," added Pam.

"I bet there are great kids in Reston," said Lulu. "I still think you should try living there."

Sandy shook her head. "I'm not moving to Reston and I need your help to get back to Powell."

Sandy tried to stand. She winced with pain. It hurt so much that her eyes filled with tears. Lulu ran over to her. "Here," she said, "lean on me." Sandy used Lulu as a crutch and boosted herself up. She hopped forward.

We can't leave Sandy alone in the woods, thought Lulu. It would be too dangerous.

But how can we convince her to come back with us?

A Leg-up

Sandy was leaning on Lulu's shoulder. "Your ankle is bad," Lulu told her. "It's not safe for you to stay in the woods alone."

"I'll be okay," said Sandy.

"What about Raffle?" asked Pam. "How are you going to feed him or lead him to water? You can't walk."

"And if you leave him loose," said Lulu, "he could run away."

"He might even try to follow us back," added Anna.

"You should come back with us," pleaded

Pam. "For Raffle's sake."

"But Raffle doesn't want to move to Reston, either," said Sandy. "He misses Peaches." Tears seeped out of Sandy's eyes and rolled down her cheeks.

Anna went over to her. "Here," she said, "lean on me, too."

"Sandy," Lulu whispered, "look at Raffle now." Lulu pointed to Raffle and Snow White. They were sniffing each other's faces.

"Raffle's good at making new friends," said Anna.

"And you can be, too," added Lulu.

"I have an idea," said Pam. "Come back with us now. Tonight we can have a meeting—the four of us. We'll think of more ideas to solve your problem. We'll help you talk to your mother about living in Powell with Liana."

"That's better than running away," said Anna.

"I don't want to leave you here." Lulu looked worried. "I'm afraid something awful will happen to you."

"Really?" said Sandy. "What do you care?"

Lulu nodded. "I like you," she said.

"Me, too," added Pam and Anna together.

Sandy looked around at the three girls. "But how can I ride back with my bad ankle?" she asked.

"Lulu and I can make a chair for you with our hands," said Pam. "We'll carry you to the trail."

"You can't carry me all the way back to Wiggins."

"We'll help you mount Raffle when we reach the trail," said Lulu. "Then we'll all walk our ponies back to Pam's."

"I'll stay with our ponies while you carry Sandy to the trail," said Anna.

Pam and Lulu made a seat for Sandy by holding each other's wrists. Sandy held on to Anna and lowered herself on the seat of hands. She put one arm around Lulu's neck and the other arm around Pam's neck.

"One. Two. Three. Go!" said Lulu.

Lulu and Pam hoisted Sandy up. Then the human chair and its passenger moved towards the narrow path.

Anna started giggling.

"What's so funny?" asked Pam.

"You're a Pony Pal ambulance," laughed Anna.

Soon they were all laughing.

"Okay," said Pam sternly. "Let's be serious. We have work to do."

Sandy imitated Pam's stern expression. "Let's be serious," she said. "We have work to do." This made them all laugh harder.

Soon the Pony Pal ambulance was heading through the woods.

When they reached the trail, Pam and Lulu lowered Sandy down on the end of a log. Then Pam and Lulu went back to the brook to help Anna bring out the ponies.

"I really like Sandy now," Lulu told Pam. "She's a lot of fun."

"And she's smart and brave," said Pam.

"It will be easy for her to make new friends in Reston," said Lulu.

"*If* she'll move there," added Pam.

"Let's think of how to convince her to move," said Lulu.

By the time the Pony Pals came back with the ponies, they had three ideas. But first they had to get Sandy onto Raffle.

Anna held Raffle. Sandy put one hand on Raffle's mane and the other hand on the back of the saddle. Pam and Lulu put their hands around Sandy's left leg to give her a leg-up. They were careful not to touch her bad ankle.

"One, two, three, lift," recited Lulu. Sandy was lifted into the air. She threw her right leg over the saddle and sat down.

"Don't put your feet in the stirrups," warned Pam. "That would hurt."

The Pony Pals mounted their ponies. Lulu led the way followed by Sandy, Pam and Anna. It was going to take a long time to reach the Crandals'.

When they came to a wide stretch of trail they rode side by side.

"I'm sorry I caused you all this trouble," said Sandy.

"We don't mind," said Lulu. "We wanted to help you. Now we can."

The Pony Pals looked at one another. Pam nodded. It was time to try their three ideas on Sandy.

Pam went first. "I went to Reston with my mother for a horse show," said Pam. "It's a nice town and it has a lot of riding trails."

"Really?" said Sandy. "I didn't know that."

Pam told Sandy other things that she liked about Reston.

Lulu smiled at Anna. It was her turn.

"Were Willow and Raffle stable mates?" Anna asked Sandy.

"Yes," answered Sandy. "They're great friends."

"Willow and Raffle would miss one another if you don't move to Reston," said Anna.

"I didn't think of that," said Sandy.

It was Lulu's turn. "Your mother is nice," she said.

"She's all right," agreed Sandy.

"I don't have a mother," she told Sandy.

"You don't?" exclaimed Sandy.

"My mother died when I was little," said Lulu. "I love my father and my grandmother, but I wish I had a mother, too. I miss her."

"I'm sorry," said Sandy sadly. "I didn't know."

No one said anything for a while.

Lulu thought, I hope Sandy is thinking about how lucky she is to have a mother. I hope she realizes she should move with her family.

Finally, Sandy spoke. "Did you just try three ideas out on me?"

"We did," admitted Anna. "We all think you should at least try living in Reston."

"I was sad when I moved to Wiggins," Lulu said. "But when I went looking for adventure, I met Lulu and Anna. Now I think Wiggins is the best place in the world to live."

"You also have a great sense of adventure, Sandy," said Anna. "You'll make new friends, too."

"I just made some new friends," said Sandy. "And I guess it did start with an adventure." She paused. "I'll do it. I'll move to Reston."

"All *right*!" shouted the Pony Pals.

Just then Snow White whinnied softly to Raffle. Raffle answered with a friendly whinny.

"Raffle's made a new friend, too," said Lulu with a laugh.

"Will you all come and visit me in Reston?" asked Sandy.

"Sure," said Lulu. "And we'll see you and Liana at all the horse shows."

"It'll be fun to have so many new friends," said Sandy.

"Yes," said Lulu. "It will be."

Lulu looked back at Snow White. She thought, Snow White, you did a great job finding Sandy. You're my best friend of all.

Dear Reader:

I am having a lot of fun researching and writing books about the Pony Pals. I've met many interesting kids and adults who love ponies. And I've visited some wonderful ponies at homes, farms and riding schools.

Before writing Pony Pals I wrote fourteen novels for children and young adults. Four of these were honored by Children's Choice Awards.

I live in Sharon, Connecticut, with my husband, Lee, and our dog, Willie. Our daughter is all grown up and has her own apartment in New York City.

Besides writing novels I like to draw, paint, garden and swim. I didn't have a pony when I was growing up, but I have always loved them and dreamt about riding. Now I take riding lessons on a horse named Saz.

I like reading and writing about ponies as much as I do riding. Which proves to me that you don't have to ride a pony to love them. And you certainly don't need a pony to be a Pony Pal.

Happy Reading,

Jeanne Betancourt